The United States

Nevada

Paul Joseph
ABDO & Daughters

visit us at
www.abdopub.com

Published by Abdo & Daughters, 4940 Viking Drive, Suite 622, Edina, Minnesota 55435.
Copyright © 1998 by Abdo Consulting Group, Inc., Pentagon Tower, P.O. Box 36036,
Minneapolis, Minnesota 55435 USA. International copyrights reserved in all countries.
No part of this book may be reproduced in any form without written permission from the
publisher.

Printed in the United States.

Cover and Interior Photo credits: Peter Arnold, Inc., Superstock, Archive, Corbis-
Bettmann

Edited by Lori Kinstad Pupeza
Contributing editor Brooke Henderson
Special thanks to our Checkerboard Kids—Aisha Baker, Jack Ward, Matthew Nichols

All statistics taken from the 1990 census; The Rand McNally Discovery Atlas of The
United States.

Library of Congress Cataloging-in-Publication Data

Joseph, Paul, 1970-
      Nevada / Paul Joseph.
      p.   cm. -- (United States)
      Includes index.
      Summary: Surveys the people, geography, and history of the state that is known
      for the huge amounts of silver once mined there.
      ISBN 1-56239-867-9
      1. Nevada--Juvenile literature. [1. Nevada.] I. Title. II. Series: United States
      (Series)
      F841.3.J67   1998
      979.3--dc21   97-16738
                                                                                 CIP
                                                                                 AC

Contents

Welcome to Nevada

When people think of the state of Nevada, most think of Las Vegas and the desert. However, Nevada is one of the most mountainous of the 50 states. There is much more in the state than Las Vegas. There are beautiful lakes, wonderful ski **resorts**, both mountain and desert golf courses, and other scenic attractions.

Nevada is sometimes called the silver state because of the huge amounts of silver that were mined there in the late 1800s and early 1900s. Today, most **minerals** are gone, although the state is still the top **producer** of gold in the United States.

Nevada is one of the largest states. But, not many people live there. Nevada ranks seventh in size but 39th in population. **Tourists**, however, make up for the lack of people. The state of Nevada is one of the most visited states in the country.

Scenery, climate, entertainment, gambling, sports, **resorts**, ghost towns, and dude ranches have made **tourism** Nevada's biggest business.

A huge neon sign in Las Vegas, Nevada.

Fast Facts

NEVADA

Capital
Carson City (40,443 people)
Area
109,895 square miles
(284,627 sq km)
Population
1,206,152 people
Rank: 39th
Statehood
Oct. 31, 1864
(36th state admitted)
Principal rivers
Colorado River
Humboldt River
Highest point
Boundary Peak;
13,140 feet (4,005 m)
Largest city
Las Vegas (258,295 people)
Motto
All for our country
Song
"Home Means Nevada"
Famous People
Patrick A. McCarran, Howard R.
Hughes, William M. Stewart,
George Wingfield, Wovoka

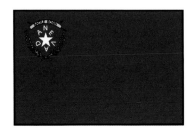

*S*tate Flag

*S*agebrush

*M*ountain
Bluebird

*S*ingle Leaf Pinon

About Nevada

The Silver State

Detail area

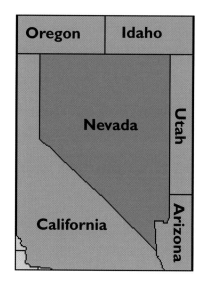

Nevada's abbreviation

Borders: west (California), north (Oregon, Idaho), east (Utah, Arizona), south (California, Arizona)

Nature's Treasures

The main reason people first began coming to Nevada was because of its treasures. There were lots of **minerals** in Nevada, like silver and gold. Today, however, the minerals are not as great, but gold, lithium, gemstones, and about two dozen more minerals are found in the state.

Other treasures include the long stretches of open range and forests. Large herds of **cattle** and sheep **graze** the ranges. More than seven million acres of Nevada is covered in forests. Some of the trees that grow there are pinon, juniper, pine, fir, and hemlock.

Nevada's climate is another treasure of the state. The Silver State is the driest of all states because the Sierra Nevada mountains cut off the rain-bearing winds from the Pacific Ocean. In northern Nevada snow falls in the mountain regions. However, it never gets too cold, which is great for skiing.

In the south it is dry with deserts and wonderful lakes. In the north there are high mountains and forests. There are also lakes, along with rivers and streams.

The great part about Nevada is that you can be skiing in the north and then drive two hours and be swimming in the south. There are not too many states with so many different natural treasures.

Black Rock Desert near Gerlach, Nevada.

Beginnings

Millions of years ago, dinosaurs roamed Nevada. Bones from the huge beasts are still found in areas around Nevada. When the land was first **explored** by **settlers** in the 1800s, many different groups of **Native Americans** were living in the area.

The first known non-Native American to have entered Nevada was missionary Francisco Garces in 1775. Also, Jedediah Smith and Peter Skene Ogden in 1828 went through Nevada. In 1848, Nevada was given to the United States by its owner, Mexico.

In 1859, the discovery of gold and silver brought a rush of people to Nevada. Cities began springing up everywhere. Virginia City was the biggest with more than 20,000 people. Today, less than 800 people live there.

On October 31, 1864, Nevada became the 36th
state to join the Union. The state had another rush of
people in the early 1900s. Silver was discovered in
Tonopah and gold was found at Goldfield.

*Millions of years ago dinosaurs roamed through what is now
southwestern United States.*

B.C. to 1848

A Wet Start

Millions of years ago much of Nevada was covered in water. Dinosaurs roamed the region.

Many years later several different groups of **Native Americans** lived in Nevada. There were the Shoshone, Northern Paiute, Southern Paiute, and Washoe, among others.

1775: Francisco Garces, on his way to California, was the first non-Native American to go through Nevada.

1848: Nevada is claimed by the United States from Mexico.

Nevada

B.C. to 1848

1861 to 1902

A United State

 1861: The Nevada Territory is created.

 1864: Nevada becomes the 36th state on October 31. Carson City is the Capital.

 1900: Silver mines are discovered.

 1902: Gold is discovered in Goldfield.

Nevada

1861 to 1902

1931 to 1992

Bright Lights, Big Cities

 1931: Gambling becomes legal in Nevada. The cities of Reno and Las Vegas grow fast.

 1936: The Hoover Dam is complete.

 1954: People discover oil in Railroad Valley.

 1992: Las Vegas native, Andre Agassi, wins the Wimbledon Tennis Tournament.

Nevada

1931 to 1992

Nevada's People

There are about 1.2 million people in the state of Nevada. There are 38 states that have more people than the Silver State. The state grew very fast when gold and silver were discovered. Since then it has been one of the least populated states. Today, however, it is getting another rush of people. Las Vegas is one of the fastest growing cities in the country.

Although the state is small, many famous people have made Nevada home. Patrick A. McCarran was born near Reno in 1876. He was a justice on the Nevada Supreme Court. He was a United States **senator** from 1933 to 1954 and sponsored many bills that helped Nevada and the rest of the country.

Old Winnemucca was the Chief of the Northern Paiutes. He signed one of the first treaties with **settlers** in western Nevada. His daughter, Sarah Winnemucca, was also well known for her work in bringing the white **settlers** and **Native Americans** together peacefully.

Many famous entertainers have made Las Vegas home, like magicians, singers, dancers, and sports stars. Elvis Presley had a home in Las Vegas. Wayne Newton, Siegfried and Roy, and tennis great Andre Agassi all live in Las Vegas.

Elvis Presley

Andre Agassi

Splendid Cities

The state of Nevada does not have many large cities. Only two, Las Vegas and Reno, have more than 100,000 people.

Las Vegas, located near the southern tip of Nevada, is one of the most visited and well-known cities in the country. There are close to 300,000 people living in the city. With visitors, there can be close to a million people in the city.

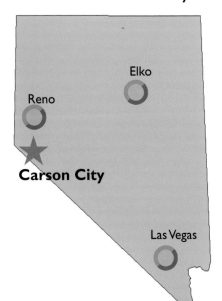

It is a booming **tourist** and entertainment center. It has huge hotels that can hold thousands of people. There are hotels like the MGM Grand that have a theme park with rides. The Treasure Island Hotel has live pirate fights in front of the hotel. Another hotel looks like a pyramid.

Most people visit Las Vegas for the gambling, golf, and entertainment. But it is also the gateway to the Lake Mead Recreation Area. Many people live and are moving to Las Vegas for the weather and jobs.

Reno is the second largest city in Nevada. The snowy mountains make for good skiing in the city.

Reno, Nevada.

Nevada's Land

Nevada's land looks very different from top to bottom. It has snow-topped mountains. Deserts and forests spread out over the land. It has lakes, rivers, dams, and streams. The land is divided into three regions.

The Great Basin covers almost the whole state. Hundreds of mountain ranges sprawl across this area. In the valleys of the mountains are stretches of ranches, farms, and dry deserts.

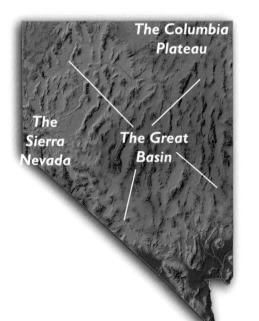

The Columbia Plateau

The Sierra Nevada

The Great Basin

The Humbolt River, the longest in the state, flows from east to west across the northern part of the state. The highest point in the state is also in this region. Boundary Peak is 13,140 feet (4,005 m) tall.

The Columbia Plateau is a region along the northeastern edge of the state. It is part of the land that comes from the region mostly in Idaho and Oregon.

The other small region is the Sierra Nevada. Most of this region is found in California. The part in Nevada is in the far western corner of the state. It overlooks Lake Tahoe on the Nevada-California border.

Fire State Park, Nevada

Nevada at Play

There are not many states with more places to play than Nevada. The people who live in the state and the millions of **tourists** who visit each year have many different choices.

Las Vegas and Reno attract thousands of visitors each day. People come to these towns to have fun at the hotels, restaurants, clubs, and casinos. Near Las Vegas is Lake Mead and the Hoover Dam.

In Reno, people can do the same things as Las Vegas. In the winter months people down-hill and cross-country ski.

Nevada has two national monuments. One is Death Valley, which extends into California. The other is the Lehman Caves, in Great Basin National Park.

The state also has many interesting ghost towns. The most popular in Nevada is Virginia City. Nevada also has many museums and excellent parks.

Skiing in Lake Tahoe, Nevada.

Nevada at Work

The people of Nevada must work to make money. Serving vacationers and **tourists** is the biggest **industry** in Nevada and employs the most people. About 400,000 of the state's 640,000 jobs deal with **tourism**.

Most of the jobs for tourism are service jobs. Service is cooking and serving food, working in stores, hotels, **resorts**, and restaurants.

People first came to Nevada to strike it rich in silver and gold **mining**. Today, **mineral** production remains a big industry. The state is still the largest **producer** of gold in the United States.

Many people in the state work in farming. More than half of the state's farming income comes from the **cattle** and calves industry. Milk, sheep, wool, pigs, and eggs also bring in a lot of money. The major **crops** in Nevada are alfalfa, hay, potatoes, wheat, and barley.

There are so many different things to do in this beautiful state. It is no wonder that it is a very fast growing state. Because of the beauty, people, land, mountains, lakes, and entertainment, Nevada is a great place to visit, live, work, and play.

Twin Creeks Mine, Nevada.

Fun Facts

•Nevada takes its name from a Spanish word meaning "snow-covered," which is talking about the higher mountain ranges in the state where snow sometimes remains all year.

•The highest point in Nevada is Boundary Peak. It is 13,140 feet (4,005 m) tall. The lowest area is the Colorado River. It is only 470 feet (143 m).

•Nevada is the seventh largest state. Its land covers 109,895 square miles (284,627 sq km).

•Lake Mead was created in 1936 because of the completion of Hoover Dam.

The Hoover Dam

Glossary

Cattle: farm animals such as cows, bulls, and oxen.

Crops: The fields of plants that farmers grow, like corn, wheat, or cotton.

Explorers: people who travel to find out more about places not many people have been before.

Graze: animals eating grass and plants.

Industry: types of business.

Minerals: things found in the earth, such as rock, diamonds, or coal.

Miners: people who work underground to get minerals.

Mining: working underground to get minerals.

Native Americans: the first people who were born in and occupied North America.

Produce: to make.

Reservation: an area of land where Native Americans live, work, and have their own laws.

Resort: a place to vacation that has fun things to do.

Senator: one of two elected officials from a state that represents the state in Washington, D.C. There they make laws and are part of Congress.

Settlers: people that move to a new land and build a community.

Tourism: an industry that serves people who are traveling for fun.

Tourists: people who travel for pleasure.

Internet Sites

State of Nevada Homepage
http://www.state.nv.us/
This site has many interesting things to see including education, sports, and entertainment all having to do with Nevada.

eNVy in the Desert
http://www.state.nv.us/gov/envy/index.shtml
(New chapters added every week to both Clark and Washoe Counties!)
A progressive novel written by Governor Bob Miller and the students of Clark and Washoe Counties.

These sites are subject to change. Go to your favorite search engine and type in Nevada for more sites.

PASS IT ON

Tell Others Something Special About Your State

To educate readers around the country, pass on interesting tips, places to see, history, and little unknown facts about the state you live in. We want to hear from you!

To get posted on ABDO & Daughters website, e-mail us at "mystate@abdopub.com"

Index